A Grasshopper in My PEAS

by Vanessa Betts

Illustrated by Brian Sams

To order additional copies of this book, contact:
Xlibris
1-888-795-4274
www.Xlibris.com
Orders@Xlibris.com

Thank you Ron. You have helped me to discover things that I never thought I would try. You bring joy and adventure to my life. The stories I share allow me to reminisce the challenges and joys of motherhood. If it wasn't for your encouragement and support, these stories would only be dinnertime conversations of yesteryear'.

A Grasshopper in My Peas

by Vanessa Betts

Illustrated by Brian Sams

All of us kids liked fruits and vegetables. Dad was always bringing home something new for us to taste. "Try it," he would say, "then you will know if you really like it or not. If someone offers it to you, you will be able to tell him or her honestly what you think about it," said Dad.

Dad ate all sorts of fruits and vegetables and most of the time

he ate them raw. "This is the way that God intended for things to be," he said.

Mom on the other hand enjoyed meat. Our vegetables were just a side dish that added color to our savory steak, chicken or pork chops. It was all about color. If we had pork chops and mashed potatoes with gravy, she had to serve beets or a green vegetable. I don't know why, she just did.

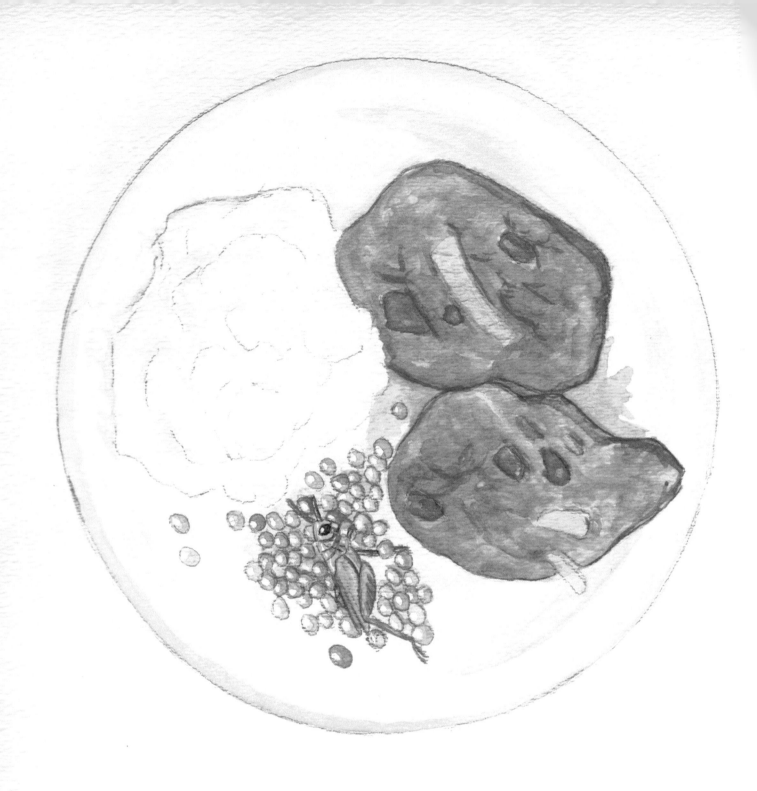

Dinnertime was a very special time. After Dad blessed the food, we all quickly tried to see who would be the first one to share something exciting about their day.

I was usually the first one to get my words out,

but nothing exciting had happened today.

Even though Mom did not care for many fruits, she insisted that we eat all of our vegetables. She made them look and smell delicious. "Eat all of your peas," she exclaimed.

"I hate peas"!

"Don't say that you hate them if you haven't even tried them," said Mom. "I have tried them and I hate them." "Still don't say you hate them son. Just say that you don't care for any," Mom said.

"Look!", I yelled.

"There's a grasshopper in my peas"! Everybody looked to see if I was telling the truth.

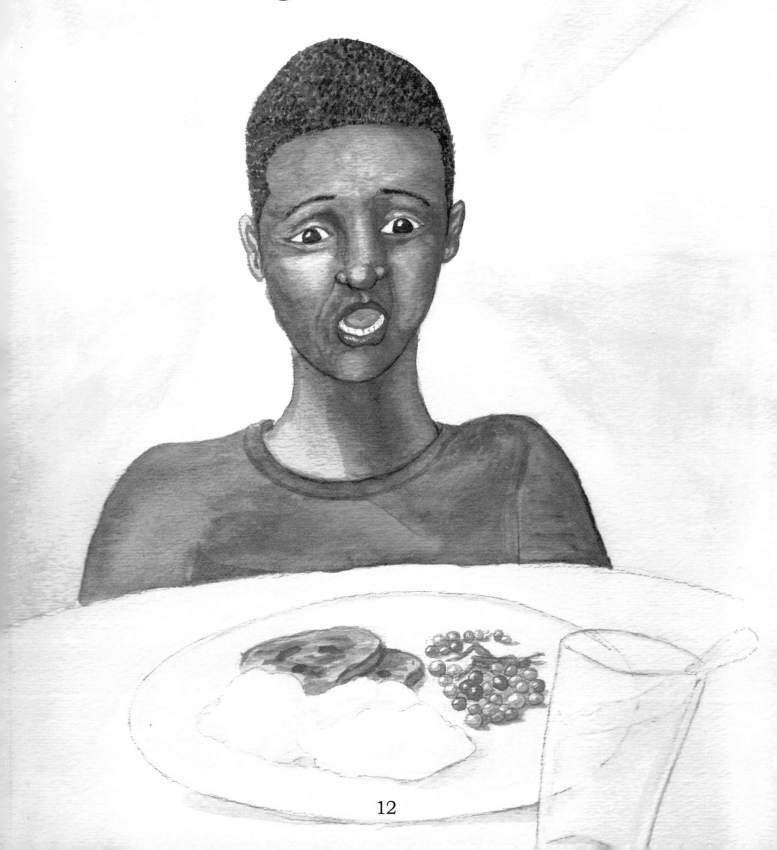

"There it is," I said as I pointed to it. It was green and seasoned with the butter sauce of the peas.

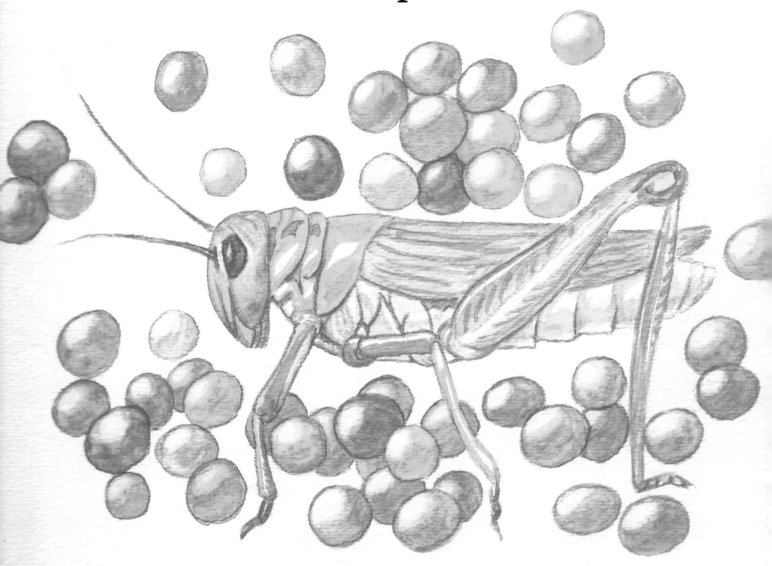

"Yuck!"

said my brother and sister.

Dad looked at the insect and said, "Those must be some pretty fresh peas because that critter blended itself right in with the rest of the green stuff from the vine."

I replied, "I don't care I'll never eat peas again." "Me either," said my older brother. "Me either," said my sister. Dad said that we were being silly. "Things like this happen sometimes," Dad said. Mom remained quiet but I think that she had decided that she didn't care for peas either.

I cook my own meals now and I try to remember Mom's color thing. When I eat out and someone offers me peas, I can honestly say, "No thank you, I don't care for any."

In my mind, I really know and remember that I hate green peas and

I hate grasshoppers.

CPSIA information can be obtained at www.ICGtesting.com
Printed in the USA
LVIW01n1411261015
459784LV00005B/7